Clippity-Clop

Other books by Pamela Allen

Mr Archimedes' Bath
Who Sank the Boat?
Bertie and the Bear
A Lion in the Night
Herbert and Harry
Mr McGee
Mr McGee Goes to Sea
Fancy That!
I Wish I Had a Pirate Suit
My Cat Maisie
Black Bog
Belinda

HAMISH HAMILTON CHILDREN'S BOOKS

Published by the Penguin Group
27 Wrights Lane, London W8 5TZ, England
Penguin Books USA Inc, 375 Hudson Street, New York, New York 10014, U.S.A.
Penguin Books Australia Ltd, Ringwood, Victoria, Australia
Penguin Books Canada Ltd, 10 Alcorn Avenue, Toronto, Ontario, Canada M4V 3B2
Penguin Books (NZ) Ltd, 182-190 Wairau Road, Auckland 10, New Zealand

Penguin Books Ltd, Registered Offices: Harmondsworth, Middlesex, England

First published in Great Britain 1994 by Hamish Hamilton Ltd
First Published in Australia 1994 by Viking Australia

Text and illustrations copyright © 1994 by Pamela Allen

1 3 5 7 9 10 8 6 4 2

The moral right of the author has been asserted

British Library Cataloguing in Publication Data
CIP data for this book is available from the British Library

ISBN 0-241-00292-3

Designed by Deborah Brash/Brash Design Pty Ltd
Typeset in 24pt Schoolbook by Post Typesetters
Made and printed in Australia by Southbank Book

Clippity-Clop

Pamela Allen

HAMISH HAMILTON • LONDON

For Tapora Betty

'Ready?' asked the little old man.

'Ready,' answered the little old woman.

'Let's go,' said the little old man.

So the little old woman pulled and pulled.
'eeeeeeeeee.......AHH!'

And the little old man pushed and shoved.
'ooooooooooo.......AHH!'

'eeeeeeeeeeee.......AHH!'

'oooooooooooo.......AHH!'
But the donkeys wouldn't go.

'So!' snorted the little old man.

'No!' yelled the little old woman.

WHACK! CRACK! went the smack.

'oooooooOOH!' cried the little old woman.

'eeeeeeeeeeeeeeOOOOOOOOOoW!'
howled the donkey.

And he was off as fast as he could go.
Clippity-clop, clippity-clop, clippity-clop,

clippity-clop, clippity-clop, clippity-clop,
clippity-clop, clippity-clop, clippity-clop.

And the little old man ran after him.
Plip-plop, plip-plop, plip-plop, plip-plop,

plip-plop, plip-plop, plip-plop, plip-plop.
And the little old woman was left far behind.

At last the donkey couldn't run any more.
He was huffing and puffing, sucking and blowing —

The little old man caught the donkey,
but this time he took a carrot from the sack
and softly began to sing.

'Yummy yummy yum-yum,
Yummy yummy yum-yum,
Come, come, come...
Come, come, come...'

Listen.......!

'Munchy crunchy lunch munch... Munchy crunchy lunch munch...
Munch, crunch, lunch............ Munch, crunch, lunch...........'

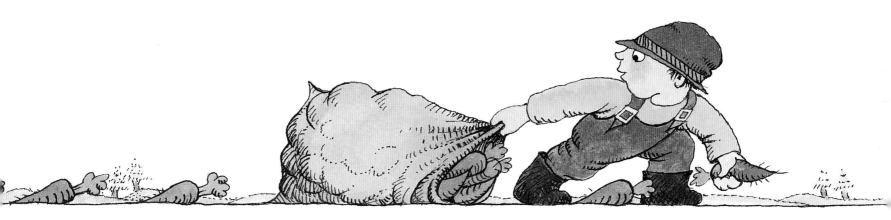

'*Yummy yummy yum-yum,*
Yummy yummy yum-yum,
Come, come, come...
Come, come, come...'

'Munchy crunchy lunch munch ... Munchy crunchy lunch munch ...
Munch, crunch, lunch .... Munch, crunch, lunch ....'

BUU............uuRRP!

Now the little old man was huffing and puffing, sucking and blowing, sucking and blowing —

Listen!   What can you hear?

Clippity-clop, clippity-clop, clippity-clop... clippity-clop, clippity-clop, clippity-clop,

clippity-clop, clippity-clop, clippity-clop,
clippity-clop, clippity-clop, clippity-clop,

clippity-clop, clippity-clop, clippity-clop,
the little old woman...

... went past like a shot!
Clippity-clop, clippity-clop, **CLIPPITY-CLOP!**